THE UGLY PLACE

4009017

Let the breeze calm your heart and the tides clear your head, and the saltwater air always remind you to stand firm and strong in your boots. *Ingirravugut suli.* Big feelings are only temporary.

Sincerely,

Laura

PUBLISHED BY INHABIT MEDIA INC.

www.inhabitmedia.com

Inhabit Media Inc. (Iqaluit) P.O. Box 11125, Iqaluit, Nunavut, X0A 1H0

Design and layout copyright © 2022 Inhabit Media Inc.
Text copyright © 2022 Laura Deal
Illustrations by Emma Pedersen © 2022 Inhabit Media Inc.

Editors: Neil Christopher and Anne Fullerton
Art Directors: Danny Christopher and Astrid Arijanto

This project was made possible in part by the Government of Canada.

We acknowledge the support of the Canada Council for the Arts for our publishing program.

Printed in Canada

ISBN: 978-1-77227-432-5

Library and Archives Canada Cataloguing in Publication

Title: The ugly place / by Laura Deal ; illustrated by Emma Pedersen.
Names: Deal, Laura, author. | Pedersen, Emma, 1988- illustrator.
Identifiers: Canadiana 20220218862 | ISBN 9781772274325 (hardcover)
Subjects: LCGFT: Picture books.
Classification: LCC PS8607.E238 U35 2022 | DDC jC813/.6—dc23

THE UGLY PLACE

by Laura Deal

illustrated by Emma Pedersen

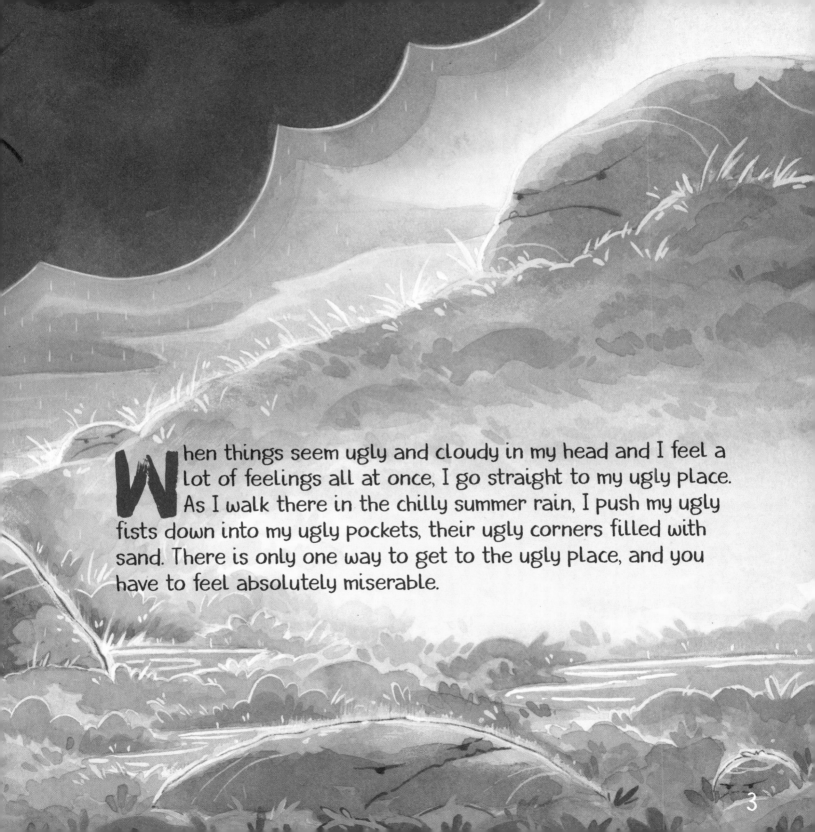

When things seem ugly and cloudy in my head and I feel a lot of feelings all at once, I go straight to my ugly place. As I walk there in the chilly summer rain, I push my ugly fists down into my ugly pockets, their ugly corners filled with sand. There is only one way to get to the ugly place, and you have to feel absolutely miserable.

I like to go when the weather is also ugly. When the clouds are grey and dark, and the raindrops plummet to the ground so heavy you can hear them. They bounce off the land, keeping time with my jittery heart.

Nothing feels beautiful today. It's just

UGLY.

I like it best when the emerald-green waters are pulled back from the land, at the lowest tide.

The mud is deep . . . and brown . . . and

SLOPPY.

The rocks are slimy . . . and cold . . . and

SLIPPERY.

Trust me, the place is so ugly that even the fish there are ugly. And the slow-moving sea snails barely move to get out of my way. There is no shining sun, not a hint of blue sky, and absolutely no colourful rainbows allowed.

THE UGLIER, the better.

My ugly, stompy footsteps leave ugly, mucky footprints, and my boots

SLURP and SLOSH

across the wet tundra. I look back over my shoulder to see the muddy trail I've left behind me. I can smell the salt water and stale seaweed.

Then, with the water now in front of me, I finally look up from the ground.

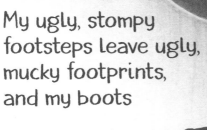

It is just as ugly as I expected.

It's perfectly ugly . . . for my perfectly

UGLY MOOD.

A seagull flying overhead lets out a long call that echoes off the hills. I kick at the puddles and I thrash and splash through the tide pools, making lots of noise. I'm soaked to my knees as the snails around me take cover in their shells.

But, for a moment, my heart settles when I see the seagull circle around again in effortless flight, joined by another. Their crisp white feathers are exceptionally bright against the sunless sky. They play while gliding and swooping through the air.

I stand still and close my eyes. My senses are finely tuned to the shoreline around me. I listen to the sound of the waves lapping steadily against the rocks as the tide begins to turn.

It reminds me to breathe deeply,

IN and OUT.

The comings and goings of my breath match the water's movements. I lick my lips and savour the taste of the salt water that has dried there.

I open my eyes again, and I can feel warmth from the sun that has just begun to make its appearance. I begin to feel more content.

Then, and only then, is when

IT HAPPENS. . . .

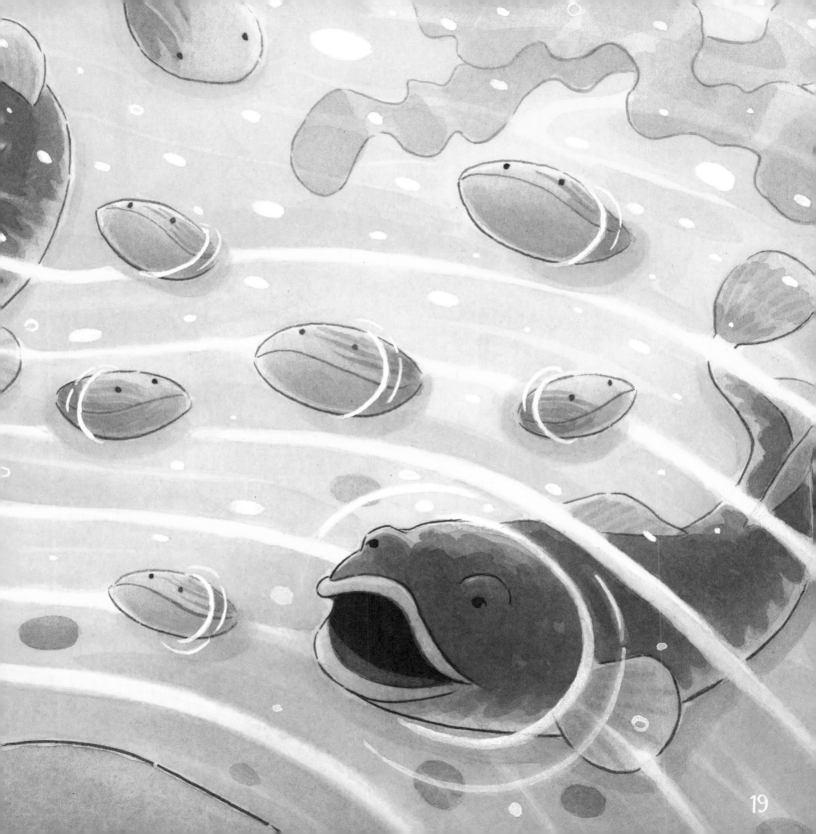

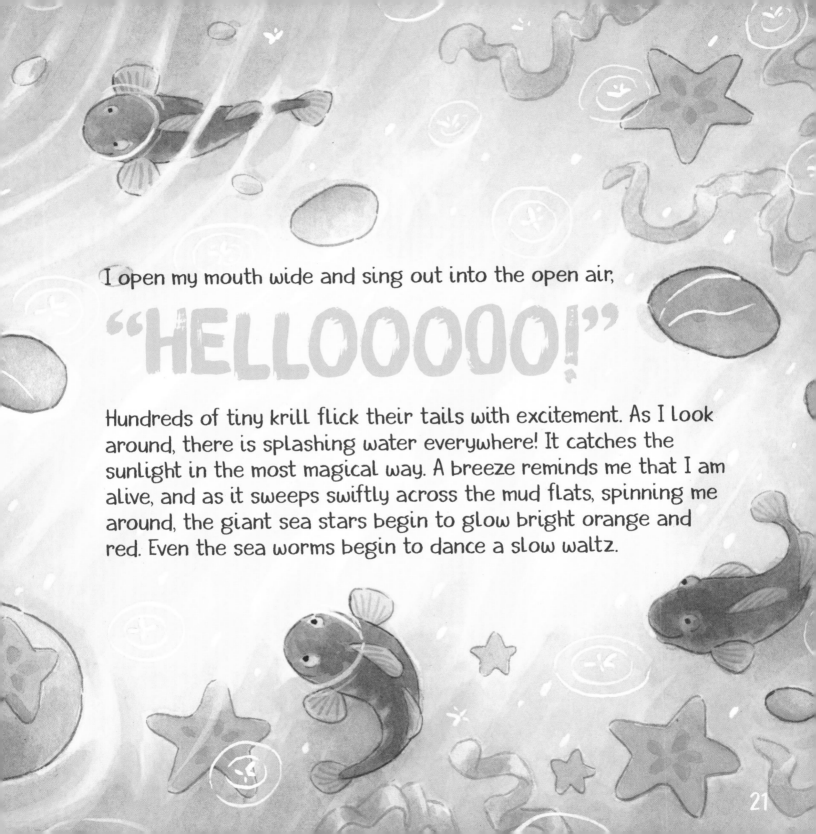

I open my mouth wide and sing out into the open air,

"HELLOOOOO!"

Hundreds of tiny krill flick their tails with excitement. As I look around, there is splashing water everywhere! It catches the sunlight in the most magical way. A breeze reminds me that I am alive, and as it sweeps swiftly across the mud flats, spinning me around, the giant sea stars begin to glow bright orange and red. Even the sea worms begin to dance a slow waltz.

I stand firm with my boots sunk deep in the sand and my arms outstretched like I'm conducting an orchestra.

A GRAND PERFORMANCE,

here and now, just for me!

And in this very moment, I can't help but

SMiLE . . .

because not a single thing around me feels ugly anymore.

Laura Deal lives in Iqaluit, Nunavut, and is originally from Musquodoboit, Nova Scotia. For her, writing has always been an important means of expression. Her Northern-based storybooks are written with the hope that children who live in the North, like her daughter, can relate and see a little bit of themselves within their pages. Laura is the author of *In the Sky at Nighttime* and *How Nivi Got Her Names*, which is also available as a short film.

Emma Pedersen is an illustrator from Toronto working primarily in children's publishing. She graduated from OCADU with a major in drawing and painting. She is also a graduate of Sheridan College's illustration program. When not working (which is rare!), she enjoys visiting used bookstores, planning her next trip abroad, and snuggling with her dog, Dolly.

It starts as a gentle stir and
a whir in the water. An overture from
under the rocks as sculpins begin to flip
and flop, tossing water into the air to announce
my arrival. A crescendo of clams emerges from the
sand. They poke out to see my face, which even I must
admit now feels a little bit less ugly.

The land and the sea life here remind me that there
are many places to find beauty. Even in the ugliest
conditions, we can make something

BEAUTIFUL TOGETHER.